*For Marguerita Rudolph (1908–1992)*

*Teacher, writer, friend of life*—AHS

*For my sister Marilyn*—GC

R01028 83984

Text copyright © 1994 by Ann Herbert Scott
Illustrations copyright © 1994 by Glo Coalson
Published by Philomel Books, a division of The Putnam & Grosset Group.
200 Madison Avenue, New York, NY 10016. All rights reserved.
This book, or parts thereof, may not be reproduced
in any form without permission in writing from the publisher.
Philomel Books, Reg. U.S. Pat. & Tm. Off.
Published simultaneously in Canada.
Printed in Hong Kong by South China Printing Co. (1988). Ltd.
Book design by Gunta Alexander. The text is set in Bryn Mawr.
Library of Congress Cataloging-in-Publication Data
Scott, Ann Herbert. Hi /by Ann Herbert Scott ;
illustrated by Glo Coalson.    p.    cm.
Summary: While waiting in line with her mother
at the post office, Margarita greets the patrons who
come in carrying different types of mail.
[1. Postal service—Fiction.] I. Coalson, Glo, ill.
II. Title. PZ7.S415Hi   1994 [E]—dc20   91-42978   CIP   AC
ISBN 0-399-21964-1
1  3  5  7  9  10  8  6  4  2
First Impression

# Hi

Ann Herbert Scott

Illustrated by

Glo Coalson

Philomel Books
New York

Margarita and her mother wrapped
a present for Margarita's grandmother
and took it to the post office to mail.
  They opened the big post office door
and found a long line of people.
  "Hi!" waved Margarita.

But nobody waved back. Nobody even noticed Margarita was there.

After a while the post office door
swung open. In came an old man
reading a newspaper.
"Hi!" called Margarita.

But the old man didn't notice
Margarita. He was too busy reading
his newspaper.

The door swung open again. Three
girls hurried in to mail some postcards.

"Hi!" said Margarita.

But the girls didn't hear Margarita.
They were too busy talking with
each other.

After a while the door swung open
again. In came a mother carrying a
crying baby.
"Hi!" said Margarita.

But the mother didn't see Margarita.
She was too busy taking care of
her baby.

The door swung open for a boy with a
tall pile of packages.

"Hi!" said Margarita, but not quite as
loud as before.

But all the boy could see were his
packages.

At last Margarita and her mother
came to the front of the line.

Margarita's mother lifted her up so she could give her package to the post office lady.

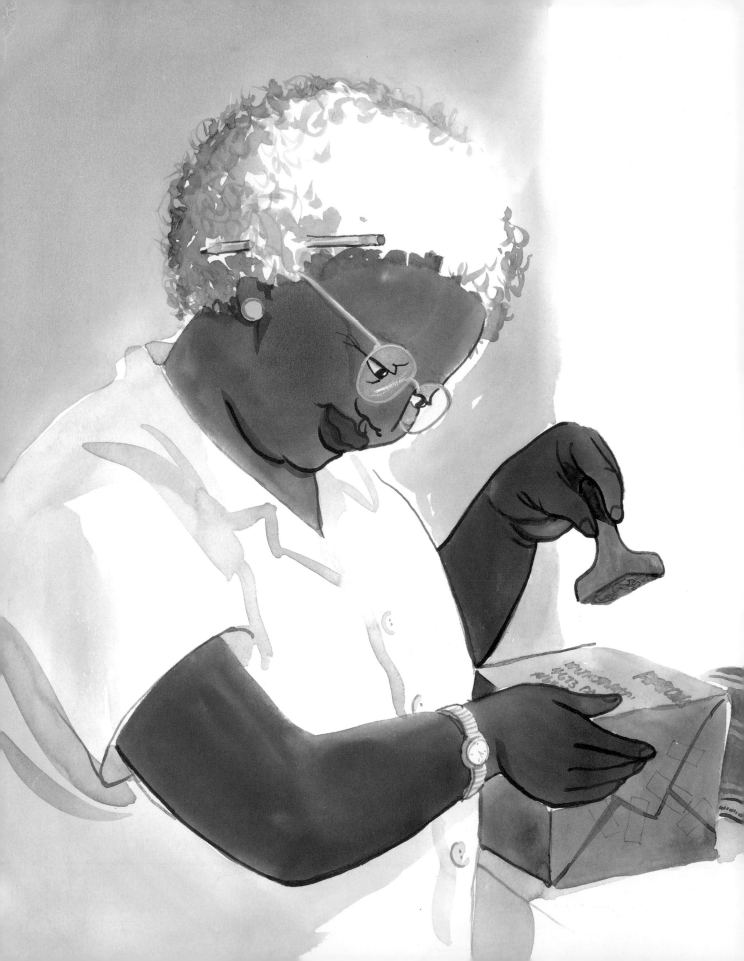

"Hi," whispered Margarita.

"Hi!" answered the lady, smiling right at her.

Margarita and her mother turned to go home.

"Bye!" said the post office lady with a big wave.

"Bye!" answered Margarita, waving back. And "Bye! Bye! Bye!" she called all the way to the post office door.